CW00833462

JERRY'S GREAT ESCAPE

By

Barbara Goulden

Illustrations by Jake Biggin

1

Copyright

Jerry's Great Escape
Text copyright © Barbara Goulden 2022.
Illustrations copyright ©Jake Biggin
All Rights reserved.

Independently Published
Paperback edition
ISBN 9798362191498

For Ellie, Pippa, Arlo and Ivy.

Katy
Above The Floor

My mum thinks my pet hamster, Jerry,
is boring and lazy. That's because she
only ever sees him when he's curled up,
fast asleep, at the top of his look-out
tower.

Mum doesn't know our secret. And I don't really think I should tell you either...

Oh well, all right.

Perhaps I will.

But like they are always saying on television – this is NOT something you should try at home.

I'm Katy by the way. My pet hamster, Jerry, lives in a crazy cage with lots of tunnels running off in all directions.

When we first got him, I kept begging Mum to buy extra bits of see-through tube so I could make his Hamster World more exciting.

One night, when I was half-asleep, I saw Jerry pushing up the lid on the newest piece of tunnelling and squeezing right out.

It wasn't easy. His cheek pouches were bulging out on either side of his face like two great big shopping bags.

Before I could climb out of bed he'd dashed across the floor to the fireplace and disappeared behind my spider plant.

I searched and called out. But all I heard was a scuffling noise underneath the floorboards.

Jerry
Below The Floor

I could hear Katy calling me as I nosed down through the cobwebs and dust beneath her bedroom floor.

She is a kind gentle little girl and I wish there was some way of telling her that I'd be back by the time she woke up tomorrow morning.

She doesn't know that ever since last Christmas I've been making my escape through a tiny hole I've gnawed in the floor behind the spider plant.

It's the first time Katy's ever seen me heading out alone. The trouble came about because I was in too much of a hurry and she was not quite asleep. Still, it's too late now.

Just need to walk this plank and slide past the hot water pipe. I can smell something delicious!

"I've got to go, Katy, I've got to go..."

Katy
Above The Floor

I was so scared Jerry would be lost forever because I already knew what had happened to Wayne Roberts' pet hamster.

You see all the houses on our street are joined together and Wayne only lives two doors away from me.

He says he wants to be the first man on Mars. The planet, not the chocolate bar.

Wayne says Jerry is just an ordinary golden hamster that's escaped from Syria, but that his dark-haired one had come all the way from Russia.

He's just telling stories because I know both of them came from the pet shop in town.

Wayne lives with his Aunty Janice and Uncle Bob and they are all mad about space travel.

He told me their hamster was a girl, so they'd called her Valentina because Aunty Janice said that was the name of the first Russian space woman.

Wayne says they're called cos-mo-nauts over there. I don't think I believe that either. He's such a show off.

Still, I did feel sorry for him when he lost Valentina. One of his friends had called round so he ran downstairs and must have forgotten to close one of the air locks on the cage properly. (They don't really lock out the air).

When Wayne got back to his room there was no sign of Valentina. But sitting beside the open cage, licking its paws, was their cat, Buzz.

Jerry
Below the floor

The delicious smell grew stronger and stronger as I reached my second home in the narrow gap underneath Katy's floorboards, and above the ceiling of the big, warm kitchen downstairs.

It is here my brave little Valentina now lives...the first hamster to journey into the space beneath the floorboards.

And with her live our three children, the twins Gerta and Boris and our new baby, Vladivostock.

When careless Wayne left Valentina's cage door open, she couldn't resist popping out to have a little sniff around. Next minute she was running for her life to avoid the claws of his cat.

But Valentina was clever. Some weeks earlier she'd discovered a hole in a rusty old water pipe. Now, in a panic, with Buzz preparing to pounce, Valentina wedged herself into that tiny hole. It was so dark, she told me, but there was no going back.

Instead, she inched herself along for what seemed like miles before arriving under the floor of the house next door.

After that Valentina balanced along a narrow strip of wood, like a circus performer, all the way through to my house.

It was there I found her, under Katy's bedroom floor. Though by that time she was weak and hungry from her journey.

I remember the day perfectly. Katy was reading beside her bedroom fireplace – there's never a fire in there because we have central heating.

I was rolling around her floor in my exercise ball when I caught the faintest whiff of something very familiar.

It took some time for me to recognise it as the sweet aroma of damp hamster.

Katy couldn't understand why I'd suddenly become so excitable. When she lifted me out of my ball for a cuddle I kept sniffing everywhere and scratching at the floorboards.

In the end, Katy got a bit cross and plonked me back down into my latest bit of plastic tunnelling.

Ah-ha! I knew the lid on the end of this particular piece of tunnel was a poor fit. As soon as Katy went to sleep that night, I heaved and pushed until finally, I was able to make a break for it.

Immediately I raced over to the pot plant next to the fireplace. There hidden from view, I nibbled and gnawed at the floorboard until I'd made a hole just big enough for me to wriggle down and investigate.

Imagine my joy at finding Valentina, a mate for me at last.

Though she was starving half to death! Quickly I unloaded all the emergency supplies from my cheek pouches, then clambered back up to my Hamster World to collect as many slices of fresh carrot and celery as I could carry.

Now Valentina is plump and well and we are very happy. Every night I come and visit with food for her and our cheerful children.

Always, Valentina hears me coming and begins warming up some porridge oats on the light fitting over the kitchen ceiling.

Katy
Above the floor

I forgot to tell you that we've got a cat too. So you can see why I was so worried about Jerry's disappearance.

I moved the spider plant to one side and made up my mind to stay awake all night and keep one eye on that little hole next to the fireplace.

First, I closed the bedroom door to keep out Sweep - that's the name of our cat.

Mum called her Sweep because when I was a baby, and she was a kitten, she used her paws to sweep up the peas I dropped from my highchair.

Next, I looked round for something I could use as a sort of ladder.

No, no. Not a ladder for me! A tiny ladder so that Jerry would find it easier to climb back up from under the fireplace.

My toy zoo was laid out on a shelf so I carefully unclipped a bit of fencing from the elephant enclosure.

I tried to peer down the tiny hole and could hear a bit of squeaking – until the dust made me sneeze and everything went quiet.

I managed to wiggle the fence-ladder down the hole. Then I found a bit of old cheese in my school lunchbox.

I knew Jerry loved cheese and would be sure to come back once he caught the smell.

All I had to do now was wait. I climbed into bed, propped myself up with three pillows and just sat, and waited. And waited. I knew I'd have to tell Mum if Jerry wasn't back soon.

What could he be doing all this time? Perhaps our neighbours were right when they said these old houses all had mice running wild under the floors.

Perhaps these underfloor mice didn't mind Jerry not having a tail and had made him their king? Or maybe he was the mouse-town greengrocer? After all he's always carrying fresh fruit and vegetables around.

Oh dear, I'm so sleepy...

Jerry
Below The Floor

Gerta, Boris and Vladivostock nearly fell over with the blast of wind that came from that great "Atishoo" up above.

Before I arrived with the shopping, they'd been glued to a little peephole which looks down into the kitchen below.

From here they can catch glimpses of the television set Katy's mother watches when she's washing dishes or exercising on her bicycle which takes her nowhere. We hamsters know about wheels and have every sympathy.

Valentina does not approve of our children watching too much television. Of course, when the house is empty during the day, we all go downstairs to the lounge and sit on the footstool to watch our favourite cartoons.

We've been watching in comfort ever since Gerta accidentally tripped over something called a remote control and startled us all by switching on the screen.

After that the children quickly learned how to change channels. Valentina, who used to only squeak in Russian, is now on level two of the English as a Second Language podcast on You Tube.

But she is very strict and only lets the children watch for a little while before telling them: "We go out now to poop and get some fresh air in the garden."

At first, they moan and groan because they don't like climbing down the ivy plant under the lounge window.

Gerta particularly worries about low-flying pigeons.

But once she's down on the ground and munching her first dandelion flower, all that's forgotten as she loves the great outdoors. Adventurous, like her mother.

Boris prefers music and makes up songs in his head which Vladivostock tries to sing. Our baby has only just learned to speak. Now he's hard to shut up. And he picks up new words so quickly. To me these are tunes to treasure.

Katy
Above the floor

So much for staying awake all night! Next morning it was only a soft scraping noise behind my spider plant that woke me up.

Sleepily I opened my eyes to see Jerry scurrying back across the floor. He looked across and I'm sure he winked at me...before squeezing into the open end of his tube.

He was so much thinner without those great bulging shopping bags on either side of his face. I watched as he crawled back up to his look-out tower, turned round in a circle and fell fast asleep.

I crept out of bed and pressed the lid back on the tube. It did seem a bit loose. I decided not to say anything to Mum. After all, my little pet had come back.

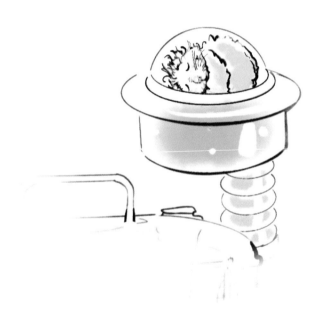

And now it's our secret. Because every night, as soon as I put my storybook down and turn off the light, I hear Jerry nudging out of that same loose tube.

I've started to leave out leftover vegetables because I just know his cheeks can always pack in more carrots and peas. I still don't like peas. Or carrots.

Every morning he arrives back at six o'clock...all "sold out."

That's my cue to get out of bed and push the loose lid back on the side of his tunnel. The good part is that when Jerry snuggles up for the day, I can climb back into my own warm bed and still have another hour and a half before I have to get up for school.

I suppose really Jerry must be some sort of mouse greengrocer. But he might be a king? Or maybe the Lord Mayor of Mice?

Whenever I stroke his lovely golden head, I always say, in a very respectful voice: "You know Your Highness, you really must be careful down there. It isn't safe."

He gazes up at me as if he understands.

Jerry
Below the floor

Very early one morning, before I climbed back up the elephant fence ladder Katy had so thoughtfully found for me, I reminded Valentina what a nice little girl she was.

"She strokes me so gently and I know she would love to meet our children."

Valentina twitched her whiskers and wrinkled her nose. "People do not always like refugees – Katy sounds very good, but she might want to keep us all in a cage," sighed Valentina.

"My love, no cage can hold you – or me," I tell her, winking at the children as they finished breakfast.

"Katy has helped us to make a good life here, even though I must go to work every day to maintain our food supply."

"You mean go to work every day to go to sleep," laughed Valentina. I watched as she carefully scraped some of the seeds out of a slice of cucumber. She hopes they will grow in a neglected part of the garden downstairs.

Boris said: "Are we refugees?"

"Not you, you were born in this country," I told him. "Although according to family tradition your great-great-great-great-great-great-great-great-great-great grandfather came from a country called Syria where he was captured by small boys who sold hamsters to tourists."

"How cruel," cried Gerta, leaving the table. She could hear Katy's mum had switched on breakfast television downstairs.

"Ah! Life can be cruel," said Valentina, firmly nudging Gerta back to the table to finish her food. "You children are a proud mixed race.

"I was watching a wildlife programme the other day and it showed dark-haired hamsters like me living underground in a land called Eastern Europe.

"I don't know how I came to live in this country but at least I am free to roam the wide-open spaces between upstairs and downstairs."

Vladivostok interrupted saying, "Daddy, Daddy, can we sing our new song? Can we, can we...?"

Listening to faint sounds of movement in the kitchen below, Valentina frowned. "No, no," she said: "It will make your father late for going back upstairs."

But I was careless and over-confident. I said, "Come on, give us a tune."

All three of our children lined up with Vladivostok in the middle and Boris picking up half a straw with holes in it which he said sounded like a saxophone.

After a quick blow the trio sang...

"Hamsters, need to be free
Hamsters, need to be free
If you put us in cages
You should pay us wages
And allow us to watch the TV."

Seven verses later, we all nuzzled noses and I set off back upstairs.

Katy
Above the floor

After a week and a half of waking up early to see Jerry safely home, I was really tired on Saturday morning and didn't hear him coming back at all.

So the loose lid on the tunnel at the far side of his Hamster World was still off when Mum came breezing into my room.

"Wake up, sleepy head," she called. "The weather forecast says it's going to be really sunny today, so I thought we'd go out somewhere for a treat."

I remember mumbling, "Great!"

Next minute I was wide-awake. Sweep had followed Mum into my room and she was snuffling all around the fireplace!

Mum didn't notice that one of the tunnels into Jerry's house was open because she was too busy complaining about the state of my bedroom. She began picking up vests and knickers and tried to shoo Sweep away from the fireplace.

But Sweep didn't want to shoo. Instead, she leapt onto the mantlepiece and stretched along the top with her head lolling over the edge.

Next, I heard the familiar little scraping noise below my spider plant and realised Jerry was preparing to scramble upstairs and into great danger.

Sweep heard the noise too. Her ears pricked up and her whole body tensed. I had to do something. And quickly.

Jumping out of bed I grabbed a handful of dried hamster food off the shelf. While stroking Sweep's head with one hand, I used the other hand to quietly dribble seeds and nuts down into the hole.

At least if Jerry was filling his cheek pouches, he wouldn't be thinking of running for a while. Sweep, of course, immediately smelled a rat – well a hamster.

It was like she knew exactly what was going on under the floor. Next thing I heard was this low, scary-sounding growl...! I didn't even know cats could growl!

Fortunately, the noise was drowned out by Mum shrieking: "Katy! What on earth is this under your duvet?"

It was one of Jerry's midnight snacks. Another bit of old cheese. But this one had started to go green. And a bit furry.

I took the cheese and tried to explain how I'd brought it upstairs on Monday but then forgotten to feed it to Jerry.

"Or he was too tired to eat it," tutted Mum, glancing across at Jerry's multi-storey Hamster World and still not realising he was missing.

Next thing we knew Sweep had jumped off the fireplace and was growling again, this time with her head pushed right through the curly leaves of my spider plant.

Jerry
Below the floor

My wise Valentina had been right. I had left it a little too late for getting back to my day job. I'd climbed half-way up the elephant fence ladder when I found myself staring right into the yellow eye of a monster!

My heart was pounding as the awful truth dawned on me. This certainly wasn't Katy. Just then, I heard a squeak from below.

It was Gerta. "Action stations! Don't worry, Dad, I'll save you!"

To my horror, Gerta had followed me to the end of the ladder and was teetering on the bottom rung. "Come back, come back," she shouted.

At the sound of her voice the monster above roared. Then a pink tongue poked through the tiny gap.

Carefully, I wobbled back to the ground. I was still wondering what to do as a mysterious shower of seeds and nuts poured down on top of me from above.

Instinctively, I begin filling my cheek pouches. You must take every opportunity to gather food wherever you find it.

"Quick, Gerta, gobble up as much as you can," I ordered. "Then go back to your mother."

"Dad, d-d-don't go back up there," stammered Gerta.

Indeed, I was about to take my daughter's advice when, as if by some miracle, I heard Katy's mother shouting, "Clear out of that fireplace you silly cat – go on, shoo!"

That was all the help I needed. Within seconds I was back up the ladder and bolting across Katy's bedroom floor, only slowed by the fact that she had left one of her trainers in the way and I had to scramble over it.

Katy
Above the floor

Jerry was making a headlong dash for his tunnel when something terrible happened! I realised I'd scattered too much food down the hole. His cheek pouches were bulging out so much he couldn't squash his head back into the narrow tube to get into his cage.

His little legs were kicking and scraping. I've never moved so fast in my whole life. Jerry's back legs were just centimetres from Sweep's open jaws when I managed to snatch him out of his tunnel, then wedge him back in, bottom first.

Instead of juicy hamster all poor Sweep got was a mini hailstorm of seeds straight into her face, as Jerry instantly slimmed down and slid to safety.

Quietly, I pressed the lid back on his tunnel as Mum finally finished tidying and turned to see our very sorry-for-herself cat desperately trying to wash her face.

She sighed and said: "Let's see if I can spare you some cream from the fridge."

Before closing the bedroom door, Mum looked over to see Jerry settling down in the sawdust at the top of his look-out tower.

"Snoozing again, I see," she smiled before adding: "Come on, Katy, get dressed. Let's spend the day at the safari park and see some real wild animals."

I could hardly believe how Mum had completely missed Jerry's race to safety.

I pulled on my jeans and tee-shirt then had to hunt round for my missing trainer. The other shoe was still lying in the middle of the floor where it had so nearly stopped Jerry's Great Escape.

"Just coming," I said.

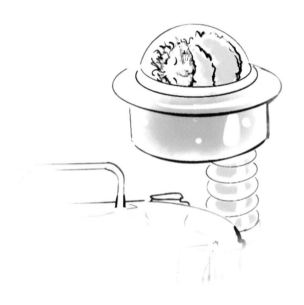

The End

About the Author

Barbara Goulden

This is the first children's book by retired journalist and grandmother Barbara Goulden who has also written two adult novels: *Knock Knock, Who's There?* and *Knocking on Haven's Door*.

Born in Manchester, Barbara now lives in Coventry with her husband Peter Walters who writes local history books.

With special thanks to Ann Evans, Katie Barker, Sophie Gardiner and Kate Walters.

Printed in Poland
by Amazon Fulfillment
Poland Sp. z o.o., Wrocław

13819442R00031